HENRY HECKELBECK

Spells Trouble

By **Wanda Coven**

Illustrated by **Priscilla Burris**

LITTLE SIMON

New York   London   Toronto   Sydney   New Delhi

This book is a work of fiction. Any references to historical events, real people, or real places are used fictitiously. Other names, characters, places, and events are products of the author's imagination, and any resemblance to actual events or places or persons, living or dead, is entirely coincidental.

LITTLE SIMON
An imprint of Simon & Schuster Children's Publishing Division
1230 Avenue of the Americas, New York, New York 10020
First Little Simon paperback edition September 2020
Copyright © 2020 by Simon & Schuster, Inc.
Also available in a Little Simon hardcover edition.
All rights reserved, including the right of reproduction in whole or in part in any form. LITTLE SIMON is a registered trademark of Simon & Schuster, Inc., and associated colophon is a trademark of Simon & Schuster, Inc.
For information about special discounts for bulk purchases, please contact Simon & Schuster Special Sales at 1-866-506-1949 or business@simonandschuster.com. The Simon & Schuster Speakers Bureau can bring authors to your live event. For more information or to book an event contact the Simon & Schuster Speakers Bureau at 1-866-248-3049 or visit our website at www.simonspeakers.com.
Designed by Leslie Mechanic
Manufactured in the United States of America 0720 MTN
10 9 8 7 6 5 4 3 2 1
This book has been cataloged with the Library of Congress.
ISBN 978-1-5344-6120-8 (hc)
ISBN 978-1-5344-6119-2 (pbk)
ISBN 978-1-5344-6121-5 (eBook)

CONTENTS

Chapter 1

SPELL CHECK

It was a quiet day at Brewster Elementary. Henry Heckelbeck opened his spy notebook and picked up a pen.

"Got any NEW secret INFO?" he asked Dudley Day.

Dudley smiled. "Yup. See that kid on the kickball field? The one at home plate?"

Henry nodded.

"Well, that kid USUALLY kicks with his RIGHT foot," Dudley explained. "But watch closely."

Henry watched the boy kick the ball. "Whoa, he just kicked with his LEFT! Good one, Dudster."

Henry made a note of it. Then he shared something he had spied. "Did you see that third grader who got a buzz cut? Now you can see where his tan line stops!"

Dudley laughed. "He has a racing stripe on his neck!"

Henry jotted down *racing stripe*.

"And guess what else?" Henry said. "Maddie Martinez forgot her new glasses today. She keeps pulling off her old pink frames and blinking a lot."

Dudley nodded. "Well, I hope she didn't lose her new frames. They have little stars INSIDE the plastic."

Henry jotted this down too.

"I have one more spy note," Dudley went on. "Your sister's teacher only took one bite of her sandwich today."

Henry scrunched his nose.
"Ew. Maybe it had MOLDY
cheese!"

That made Dudley giggle.
Then somebody *behind* them
giggled too.

It was Max Maplethorpe. She had been watching over their shoulders.

"What in the world are you doing?" Henry cried.

Max smirked. "Reading your SPY NOTES!"

Henry slapped his notebook shut. "It's a flip-flop, Dudley! The spies have been SPIED on!"

Max took a step back.

"Hey! Take it easy!" she said.
"Remember, I'm a fellow spy!
And for your information,
you misspelled three words in
your book."

"Where?" Henry asked.

"'Glasses' has three *s*'s," Max said. "And 'kickball' is ONE word—not TWO. And there's no 'WITCH' in 'sandwich.'"

Henry checked his spelling and said, "Merg! You're right!"

Max smiled and arched the bill of her baseball cap.

"Looks like you guys better brush up on your spelling," she added. "Because it's almost time for the Brewster Spelling Bee . . . and I plan to W-I-N."

Chapter 2

WORKER BEES

"Hocus-pocus! Time to focus!"
called the teacher, Ms. Mizzle.
The class became quiet.

"I have some exciting news!"
she said. "This year we will join
the Brewster Spelling Bee."

Henry slumped in his chair.
Ugh, Max was right again!

Henry did *not* like the idea of spelling words in front of other people. He looked to Dudley for help, but Dudley just shrugged.

A girl named Stella Shah raised her hand and asked, "How does a spelling bee work? And does it sting?"

"Excellent questions, Stella," said Ms. Mizzle. "First, no, a spelling bee doesn't sting. It's not a bee at all! It's a contest where students in different classes compete by spelling words!"

Stella let out a big *Phew!*

Then Ms. Mizzle continued. "Okay a spelling bee has three jobs. The word giver, each speller, and the judge. The word giver says the word to be spelled. The speller *spells* the word. And the judge decides if the word was spelled correctly. Any questions?"

Dudley raised his hand. "How much time do you get to spell a word?"

Ms. Mizzle held up two fingers. "Two minutes."

Max's hand shot up next. "Do you get a prize if you win?"

Ms. Mizzle nodded. "Yes, Max, a prize will be given for the winner in each grade."

Dudley's hand shot up again. "Where is the spelling bee going to *bee* held?"

Ms. Mizzle laughed and checked her notes.

"The spelling bee will be held on the Brewster stage. Each grade will take turns during the day. Our class will go last. Family and friends are all invited too! Isn't this *exciting*?" she said.

Then the class began to all talk at once. Henry just picked at the corner of his desk.

He did not think a spelling bee sounded exciting. It sounded *terrifying*.

Chapter 3

BEE QUIET!

Henry planted his broccoli deep into the soft part of his baked potato at dinner. Then he sprinkled shredded cheddar cheese on top of his broccoli forest.

"How was school?" asked Dad.

"Pretty good," he said. He wasn't about to mention the spelling bee.

But then his sister, Heidi, made it a news flash.

"School was BEEautiful! It's time for the Brewster Spelling Bee!" she said.

"How fun," said Mom.

"And you know what ELSE?" Heidi asked.

Mom and Dad shook their heads.

"Family and friends can come to cheer for everyone! And MORE great news!" Heidi went on. "This year *I* plan to compete!"

Mom and Dad noticed that Henry wasn't as excited as his sister.

"You're being quiet, Henry,"
Mom said. "What about you?"
"What ABOUT me?" he said,
not looking up from his plate.

Mom tried again. "Are you going to take part in the spelling bee too?"

Henry pushed his plate away. "Do I have a choice?"

Dad reached over and patted Henry on the back. "I happen to know that you are a *great* speller! You can even wear my lucky *bumblebee* bow tie! Would you do it then?"

Henry crossed his arms. "Not if I don't have to."

Heidi frowned at her brother. Then she turned back to Mom and Dad.

"Well, I'VE already started to practice MY spelling," she said. "Give me a word—ANY WORD—and I'll spell it for you!"

Dad stroked his chin. "How about the word 'crowd'? As in: We will be in the *crowd* cheering for you both."

Heidi took the saltshaker and held it like a microphone.

"Crowd," she repeated. "C-R-O-W-D. That spells 'crowd.'"

Henry knew he was doomed. There was no escape. He had to do the spelling bee whether he liked it or N-O-T.

Chapter 4

BEE-WARE!

Henry crawled into bed that night and pulled the covers over his head.

All he could think about was the spelling bee.

Soon he began to dream.

Suddenly Henry stood on a center stage—all alone. The room was dark, but Henry could see the crowd in their seats.

A spotlight switched on, and the light beamed on Henry. He covered his eyes with his arm.

Then he heard a noise.

BUZZZZZZZZ.

The spotlight moved away
from Henry and landed on a
giant bee.

The bee's face looked a little like Principal Pennypacker's— which was really weird. Plus, he had the body of a bumblebee, and he was flying!

Henry swallowed hard. "Who are YOU?" he asked.

The bee laughed loudly. "Why, I am the Spelling Bee!

I'll be your host for today's Buzzy Brewster Spelling Bee!"

The giant bee turned to face the crowd as they clapped and cheered.

"Our contestant is Henry Heckelbeck from Ms. Mizzle's class," the Spelling Bee said as he turned toward Henry. "Your word is 'mudollop.'"

The spotlight shifted back to Henry. He shoved his hands deep into the pockets of his pants.

"Is that even a REAL word?" Henry asked. His voice boomed from the speakers.

The Spelling Bee smiled and waited for Henry to spell the word.

"Can you use the word in a sentence?" Henry asked.

The bee nodded.

"Yes, you *can* use 'mudollop' in a sentence," he replied. "You see? I *just* did!"

Henry felt his face grow warm. "But can you use the word in a sentence that makes SENSE?"

The smile left the Spelling Bee's face. He stuck out his lower lip.

"Oh dear, Henry Heckelbeck from Ms. Mizzle's class," he said. "I can see that you're not ready for the spelling bee."

The whole audience gasped. "Look at Henry Heckelbeck," they chanted. "He's not ready. He's NOT READY!"

Then the Spelling Bee flew above center stage. The crowd stopped chanting.

"What's the matter with Henry?" the bee asked the crowd. "Has the cat got his tongue?" Then the crowd began to laugh and point.

Henry looked to see where they were pointing. He saw a *giant cat* creeping across the stage. Henry tried to run away. But his feet wouldn't move! It was like they were glued to the floor.

"HELP! Somebody, HELP!" he cried. "The cat's trying to get my TONGUE!"

Suddenly Henry sat upright in bed. His alarm clock was buzzing—just like a *bee*. Henry slapped the off button.

It was only a bad dream! he thought. Henry wiped his brow and realized something. The dream was fake, but the spelling bee at school was still very, very real.

And he wasn't ready.

Chapter 5

BUSY BEES

Instead of his spy notebook, Henry brought a dictionary to recess.

"Come on!" he said to Dudley. "Let's practice for the spelling bee."

Dudley followed Henry to the side of the school building. Nobody would bother them there. The boys sat down and leaned against the wall. Henry opened the dictionary to the letter *M*.

"Have you ever heard of the word 'mudollop'?" Henry asked.

Dudley shook his head. "Nope. Definitely not."

Henry ran his fingers down the pages.

"Well, last night I dreamed about the spelling bee. I got the word 'mudollop,' and I want to see if it exists." Henry tried two different spellings. But neither one was in the dictionary. "The word seemed so REAL in my dream!"

Dudley laughed. "You are so W-E-I-R-D," he said, spelling the word out.

Somebody else laughed too. The boys looked up. It was Max, of course.

"Whatcha doing, guys?" she asked.

Dudley lifted the dictionary. "We're practicing our S-P-E-L-L-I-N-G," he said. "And I just made up a new R-U-L-E. From now on, we have to spell one W-O-R-D in every sentence we say."

Max sat down in front of the boys and wrapped her arms around her knees.

"Okay," she said. "You want some H-E-L-P?"

Before anyone could answer, Max held up her hand. "Wait! I actually have some S-P-Y info to share."

Henry and Dudley leaned in closer.

She whispered, "Well, it's about Principal Pennypacker. He's wearing a Band-Aid on his F-I-N-G-E-R. But it's not just ANY Band-Aid. It's a . . . G-L-I-T-T-E-R Band-Aid."

The boys' mouths dropped open.

"Whoa, why would the principal wear a G-L-I-T-T-E-R Band-Aid?" Dudley asked.

Max shrugged. "Who knows?" she said. "But it makes him look M-A-G-I-C."

Dudley laughed and said, "A MAGIC principal? But he doesn't even have a long white beard or a pointy H-A-T!"

Then Max pinched her lips together. "I didn't say he WAS M-A-G-I-C. I said he LOOKED M-A-G-I-C."

Henry shook his head at Dudley, like *duh*. All this talk about magic was making him a little nervous. So he changed the subject.

"Are you going to H-E-L-P us or not?" he asked Max.

Max smiled as she took the dictionary from Henry.

"Y-E-S!" she said.

Chapter 6

RELAX, BEE HAPPY!

At home, Henry sat on his bedroom floor with the family dictionary. He had messy hair and dark circles under his eyes. He looked like he hadn't slept for days and days.

Heidi stood in the doorway.

"You look like a wreck," she said.

"Thanks," Henry answered without looking up from the dictionary.

Then Heidi whipped out a piece of paper from behind her back.

"Guess what I have?" she said, lifting her eyebrows. "Last year's spelling bee words for your grade. I can test you if you want."

Henry shut the dictionary.

"Really?" he asked. "That would be great!"

Heidi sat down on the floor opposite Henry. Then she read each word out loud—"cake," "bike," "crab," "kick," and "soccer."

Henry spelled every word right—even "soccer."

"See?" his sister said, folding the word list into a small square. "You have nothing to worry about."

Henry bit his lip. "It's not the SPELLING I'm worried about."

Heidi folded her arms. She knew her brother wasn't telling her everything. "Then what is it?"

"You have to promise not to laugh," Henry said.

Heidi promised. She even crossed her heart, and that was enough for Henry.

Suddenly all his fears tumbled out.

"I'm kind of scared of being onstage," he said. "What if I trip? Or what if I burp in the middle of a word? What if everyone laughs at me?"

Henry's heart was racing fast. "Or WHAT IF . . . a GIANT CAT tries to get my tongue?!"

Finally Heidi held up her hand to stop her brother.

"Whoa!" she cried. "You've got it ALL wrong! Spelling bees are FUN. They're way easier than blocking a penalty kick in soccer. And you do that ALL the time!"

Henry sat up. "Penalty kicks? I LOVE to block penalty kicks!"

Heidi smiled. "Then the spelling bee will be a snap!"

"What if I get everything wrong?" asked Henry.

"You know what happens if you misspell a word?" Heidi said. "You get to sit and watch the rest of the class!"

That doesn't sound too bad, Henry thought.

But he knew one thing for sure: He definitely didn't want a giant cat to get his tongue.

Chapter 7

BEE CALM

Henry stared at the glow-in-the-dark stars on his ceiling. He did not want to fall asleep. What if he had another bad dream? He rolled over and plumped his pillow.

Then something caught his attention.

A ball of light started to glow on his bookshelf. Henry sat forward as the glow began to float through the air . . . toward him. It was that weird old book again!

A medallion slid out of the book. The chain circled Henry's head and came to rest around his neck. Then the book landed gently in his lap and opened to a spell.

A Honey of a Spell-ing Bee

Are you the kind of wizard who thinks spelling bees are scary? Perhaps you don't like to spell words in front of other people. Or maybe you're too worried about being onstage. If you think the cat is trying to get your tongue, then this is the spell for you!

Ingredients:

1 tablespoon of honey
2 flakes of lavender soap
1 pocket-size dictionary
3 deep breaths

Mix the ingredients together in a bowl and take three deep breaths. Hold your medallion in one hand and hold your other hand over the mix. Chant the following spell.

To have a happy spelling bee,
Honey, be calm. That's the key!
Now say it out loud: "I am free!
And stage fright is no part of me!"

Note: This spell has side effects. It may attract buzzy buddies and cause old-fashioned talk. To break the spell, do something unselfish.

Henry couldn't believe his luck. This was the *perfect* spell for him—and it wasn't even cheating! The magic would only work to keep him calm.

Henry tiptoed out of bed and collected all the ingredients.

He stirred the mix, took three deep breaths, and cast the spell.

Whoosh! A feeling of peace washed over Henry, and he fell fast asleep.

Chapter 8

BEE READY

The next morning, Mom handed Henry a mixed-berry smoothie for breakfast.

"A thousand thank-yous, Mother," Henry said. "What a fine way to start the day!"

Dad reached over and put
his hand on Henry's forehead.
"Are you feeling all right?"

Henry blushed.
*The spell wasn't
kidding about side
effects,* he thought.
Then he tried to
talk normally.

"I've never been better,
Father!" Henry said in NOT
a normal way. "Do you and
Mother still plan to attend the
spelling bee today?"

Dad looked at Heidi and raised his eyebrows. Heidi shrugged and looked at Mom. Mom shook her head and looked back at Dad. So Dad played along.

"Yes, Son," he said. "Mother and I shall both attend the spelling bee this afternoon!"

Phew! Dad thinks I'm joking! Henry thought.

"You are so amusing, dear Father!" responded Henry. "I shall see you later!"

On the way to the bus, Heidi said, "Please knock off the old-timey talk, Henry. It's REALLY weird."

Henry nodded and kept his mouth shut. He didn't want his friends to hear him either. What would they think?

He decided to keep quiet until *after* the spelling bee.

Henry was silent all day. He did his math in the math corner.

He wrote his soccer paragraph alone in the library.

He ate lunch at his desk and studied his spelling words. Nobody even noticed because the whole class was studying for the spelling bee.

Finally Ms. Mizzle chimed
her triangle. "Time to line up
for the spelling bee!"

Everyone pushed back their chairs and raced to the door. Then the class filed into the auditorium and climbed the stairs onto the stage. The crowd was already seated. Henry spotted his parents and waved.

Wow, he thought. *I don't feel one bit afraid!*

The spell had worked.

Chapter 9

BEE CAREFUL!

The class sat side by side in grown-up chairs so big that no one's feet reached the floor.

Henry sat on his hands and swung his legs back and forth. He felt great.

Soon Principal Pennypacker welcomed everyone, and the spelling bee began. He called Henry's name first. Henry hopped from his seat and walked to the microphone.

"Henry, your word is 'carry,'" said the principal. "As in: Please help me *carry* these heavy books. Carry."

Henry leaned toward the microphone.

"Carry," he repeated. "C-A-R-R-Y. Carry."

Principal Pennypacker nodded.

"Very good, Henry!"
The audience clapped.
"Woo!" shouted Dad.

Then Henry swore he could hear a bumblebee buzzing in the room. *That's weird,* he thought.

He watched Dudley and Max spell the words "soggy" and "wink" correctly. After they went, Maddie Martinez spelled "coat" wrong.

"I'm sorry," said the principal. "That spelling is incorrect."

Henry watched Maddie leave the stage. She was smiling and happy and didn't seem upset at all. Plus, the audience still clapped for her! Maybe this would be easier than he had originally thought.

When they reached the final round, it was Henry against Max!

Max went first. She spelled the word "buzz": B-U-Z-Z.

And "buzz" was the right word! As soon as she finished, Henry heard a swarm of bees.

Then Henry stepped forward and saw them! There were bees buzzing above the audience.

The crowd noticed them too. People started to get up and leave!

That was when Henry remembered the note about side effects from the spell.

OH NO! he thought. *I've been talking, and honey words can bring buzzy buddies. . . . That means I'm attracting bees whenever I talk!*

Chapter 10

BEE BRAVE

Henry could not remember how to break the spell. Was there a special word? Did he need to eat honey? What was it?!

Then it came to him. Being unselfish was the key.

Henry stood in front of the microphone and knew exactly what to do.

"Okay, Henry, your next word is 'magic,'" the principal said. "As in: Sometimes *magic* can spell trouble. Magic."

Henry gulped.

Does Principal Pennypacker KNOW something? But how? There's NO way. He took a deep breath.

"Magic . . . ," he repeated.
"M-A-J-I-K. Magic."

Henry's body twitched and the buzzing hum of the bees disappeared. The spell had been broken.

Henry heard his sister and his parents gasp. Not because they noticed the spell. They just couldn't believe Henry had misspelled "magic"!

Then Max saw her chance and raced to the microphone. "MAGIC," she said loudly. "M-A-G-I-C. Magic."

The principal turned to the crowd and announced, "We have a WINNER!"

The crowd erupted with claps and cheers as Principal Pennypacker placed a medal around Max's neck.

Henry congratulated Max. "Way to go!" he said.

But Max wrinkled her nose at Henry. "Did you spell that last word wrong to help me win?"

"Why would I do that?" Henry said.

"I don't know, but I'm keeping an eye on you, Henry Heckelbeck!" Max said as she ran to her family.

Then somebody slapped Henry on the back. He turned around and saw his sister and parents.

"Great job!" Heidi cried. "I didn't even make it out of round two this year!"

"We're proud of you, Henry!" Dad said. "May we take you out to dinner tonight? Your choice."

"YES!" Henry cried. "Can we have P-I-Z-Z-A? Because I'm STARVING."

Dad winked. "In that case, we'd better *bee* going!"

"O-K!" Henry said.

And the whole family laughed because Henry had the last *word*.

Check out the next book starring

HENRY HECKELBECK

HENRY HECKELBEC
and the Race Car Derby

23

Henry Heckelbeck and his best friend, Dudley Day, raced into the backyard.

Both boys stared at the tops of the trees. They watched the leaves flutter in the wind.

An excerpt from *Henry Heckelbeck and the Race Car Derby*

"This is a PERFECT kite day," Henry declared.

"Finally!" agreed Dudley. The boys had been waiting for a windy day for weeks.

They grabbed their kites, invited Henry's dad, and then went to the park.

Henry had a green-purple-and-blue kite. Dudley had a big rainbow-colored kite that was shaped like a diamond.

An excerpt from *Henry Heckelbeck and the Race Car Derby*

At the park, the boys passed a kickball game, picnickers, and a dad playing catch with his daughter. Soon they found an open area. The boys backed away from each other so their lines wouldn't get tangled. Then they grabbed their kites in one hand and their spools in the other.

"Ready?" yelled Dudley.

Henry nodded.

An excerpt from *Henry Heckelbeck and the Race Car Derby*